The SUITORS
Princes of Ithaca, who had installed
Themselves in the court of Ulysses.
They wish to marry Penelope.

CIRCE
Goddess and enchantress, daughter of Helios.
She can transform men into animals.

CALYPSO
A goddess who lives on an island in the sea's umbilicus.
She restrains Ulysses for seven years.

POLYPHEMUS
Cyclops with just one eye in the middle of his forehead.
The son of Poseidon, king of the sea.

THE LOTUS-EATERS
A people that feeds on the fruit
Of the lotus plant.

The LAESTRYGONIANS
Giant cannibals.

THE PHAEACIANS
A navigating people.
Their magic boats can read thoughts.

HELIOS
God of the Sun. He is Circe's father.

POSEIDON
Lord of the sea.
Brother to Zeus.

Originally published as *L'incredibile viaggio di Ulisse*
© 2007 edizioni ARKA, Milan
www.arkaedizioni.it

© 2010 edizioni ARKA

First published in the United States of America in 2010
by the J. Paul Getty Museum

Getty Publications
1200 Getty Center Drive, Suite 500
Los Angeles, California 90049-1682
www.getty.edu/publications

Printed by Stampe Violato, Bagnoli di Sopra, Italy (09C0479)
Bound by LeZana Srl, Padua, Italy
First printing by the J. Paul Getty Museum (12431)

Library of Congress Control Number: 2009932972
ISBN 978-1-60606-012-4

The Incredible Voyage of
ULYSSES

This story comes down to us from ancient Greece,
Through the great poet Homer.

The ancient poets had sung it for centuries
Before it was written down and passed down
Through the ages with the title of *The Odyssey*.

It tells of the adventures of Odysseus,
Better known as Ulysses.
A simple man at the mercy of the gods, the sea,
Of giants, monsters, nymphs, and enchantresses.
A great, clever hero, daring, cautious and heedless,
Ready to face anything
And everything to achieve his goal.

I shall tell you my version
Of this odyssey,
The eternal metaphor
For every person's life.

Text and illustrations by Bimba Landmann

The J. Paul Getty Museum, Los Angeles

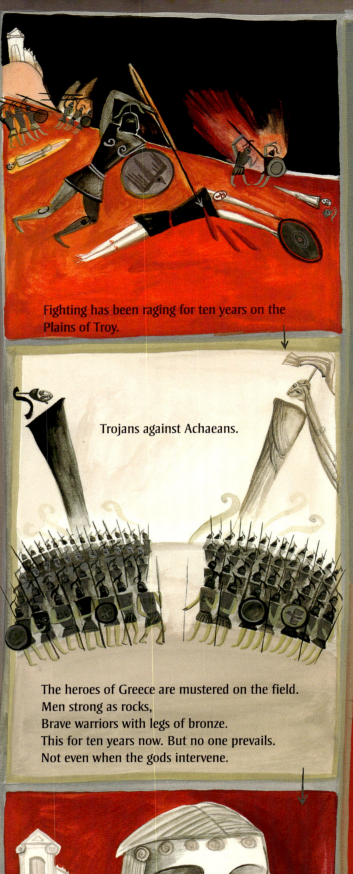

Fighting has been raging for ten years on the Plains of Troy.

Trojans against Achaeans.

The heroes of Greece are mustered on the field.
Men strong as rocks,
Brave warriors with legs of bronze.
This for ten years now. But no one prevails.
Not even when the gods intervene.

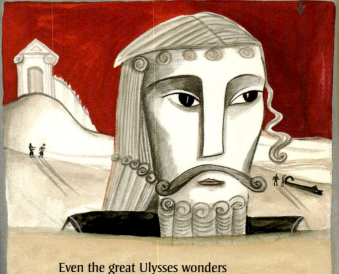

Even the great Ulysses wonders
If this war will ever end.

Until one day he discovers
A way to beat the Trojans.
Of superior intelligence,
With his sharp wits he conceives
The most famous deception in history.

Ulysses has a huge wooden horse built.
Then tricks his enemies to believe in his surrender.
His ships set sail, one after the other.
But he and his men hide in the huge horse.

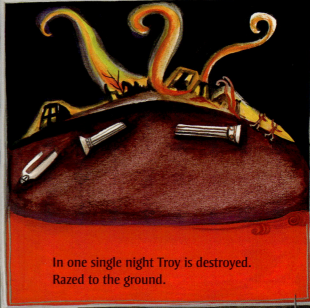

In one single night Troy is destroyed.
Razed to the ground.

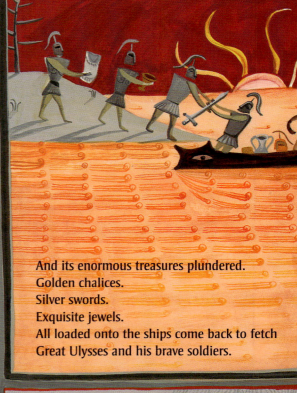

And its enormous treasures plundered.
Golden chalices.
Silver swords.
Exquisite jewels.
All loaded onto the ships come back to fetch
Great Ulysses and his brave soldiers.

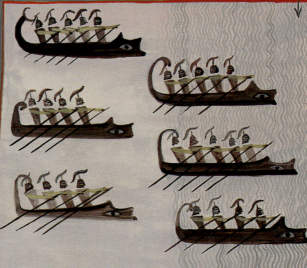

As foreseen, the Trojans pull
The horse inside the city walls.
Ulysses and his men bide their time.
Silent and still.
Night falls,
And an unnatural silence settles on Troy, too.
The Trojans sleep.
It is then that Ulysses gives the sign and all hell breaks out.

How they long to return home after ten long years!
Steadily the men row over the vast sea.

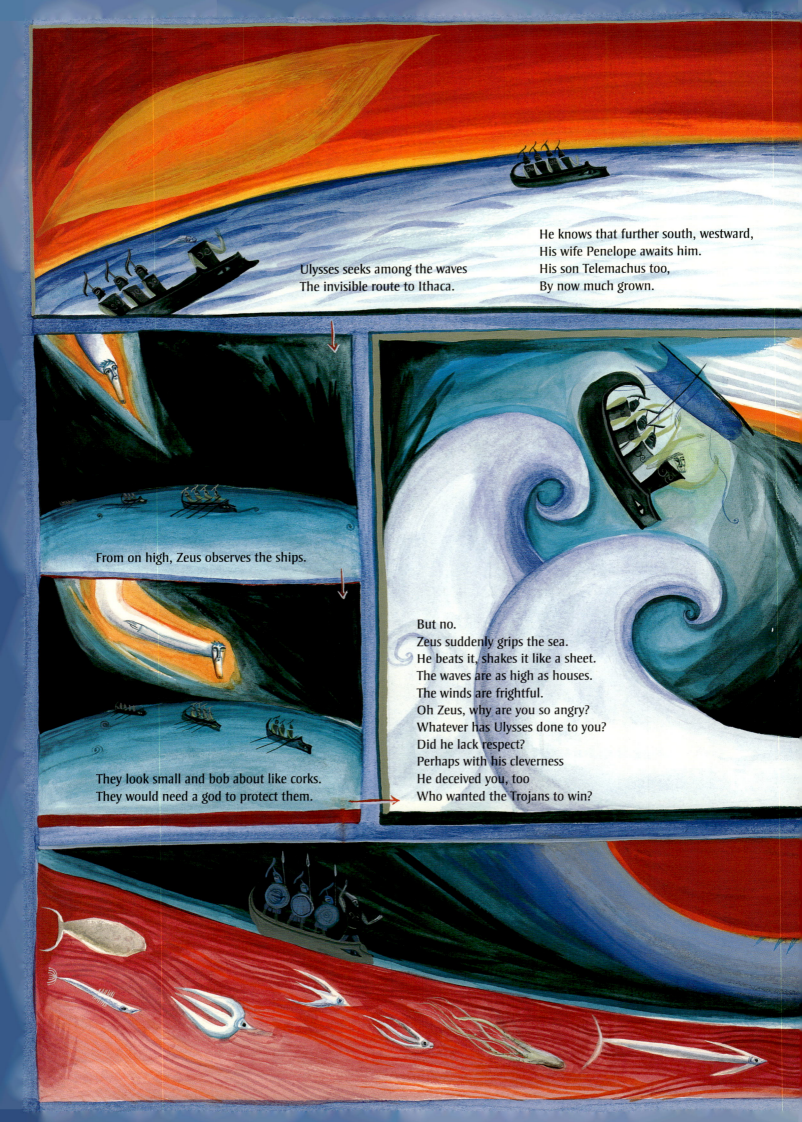

Ulysses seeks among the waves
The invisible route to Ithaca.

He knows that further south, westward,
His wife Penelope awaits him.
His son Telemachus too,
By now much grown.

From on high, Zeus observes the ships.

They look small and bob about like corks.
They would need a god to protect them.

But no.
Zeus suddenly grips the sea.
He beats it, shakes it like a sheet.
The waves are as high as houses.
The winds are frightful.
Oh Zeus, why are you so angry?
Whatever has Ulysses done to you?
Did he lack respect?
Perhaps with his cleverness
He deceived you, too
Who wanted the Trojans to win?

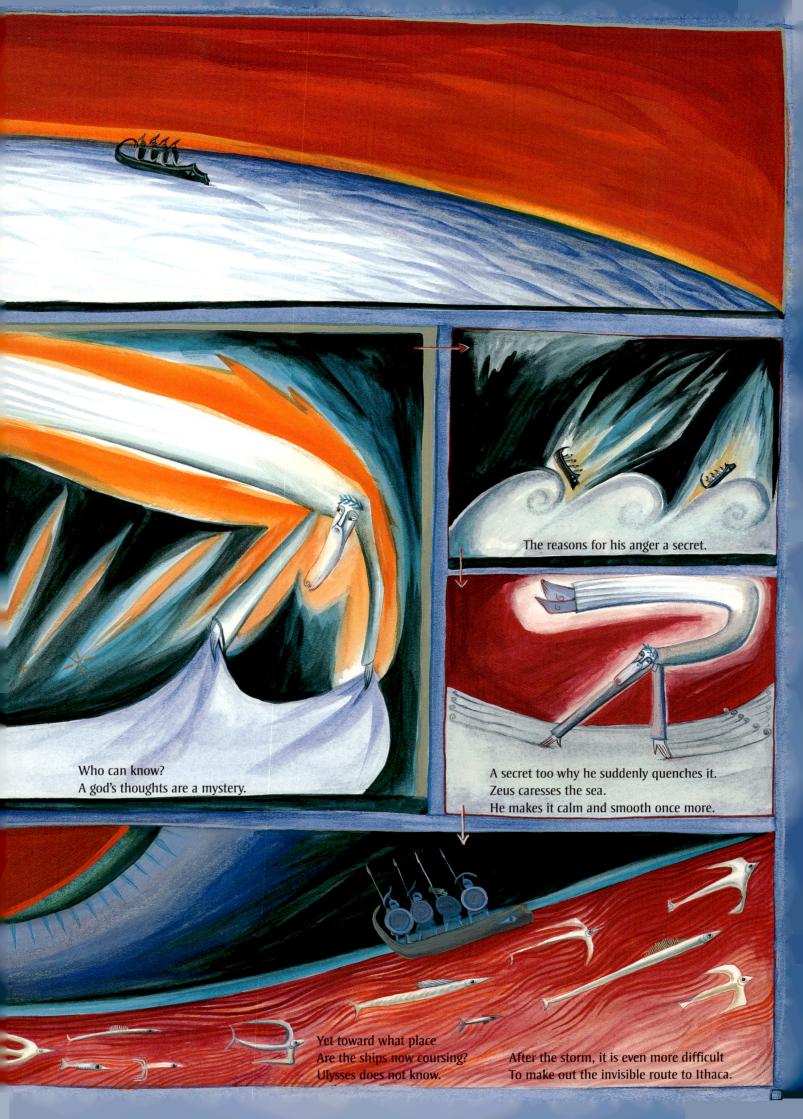

The reasons for his anger a secret.

Who can know?
A god's thoughts are a mystery.

A secret too why he suddenly quenches it.
Zeus caresses the sea.
He makes it calm and smooth once more.

Yet toward what place
Are the ships now coursing?
Ulysses does not know.

After the storm, it is even more difficult
To make out the invisible route to Ithaca.

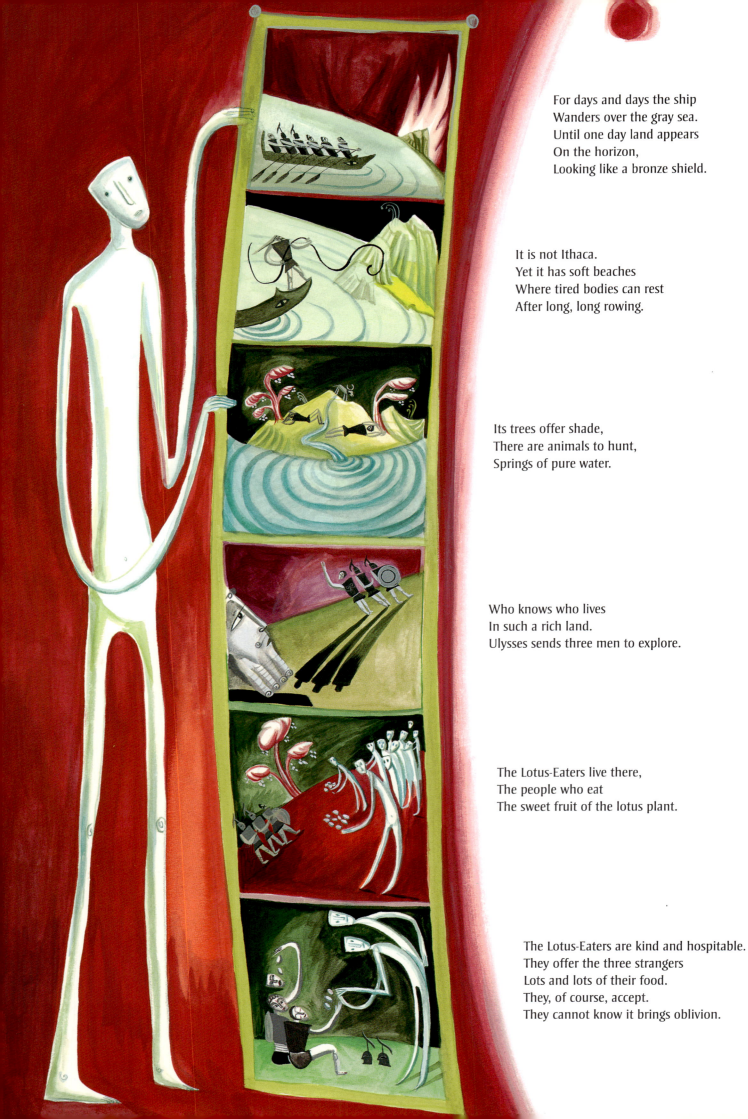

For days and days the ship
Wanders over the gray sea.
Until one day land appears
On the horizon,
Looking like a bronze shield.

It is not Ithaca.
Yet it has soft beaches
Where tired bodies can rest
After long, long rowing.

Its trees offer shade,
There are animals to hunt,
Springs of pure water.

Who knows who lives
In such a rich land.
Ulysses sends three men to explore.

The Lotus-Eaters live there,
The people who eat
The sweet fruit of the lotus plant.

The Lotus-Eaters are kind and hospitable.
They offer the three strangers
Lots and lots of their food.
They, of course, accept.
They cannot know it brings oblivion.

Slowly their minds cloud over.
It's like a rising fog
That makes them forget everything.
They forget their journey,
Ulysses, even Ithaca.

They fall to the ground,
As heavy as rocks.
And they go on eating
The treacherous lotus fruit.

When Ulysses finds them,
He has to use force to raise them.
And force to drag them away.
"Leave us alone. Who are you?
What do you want?"
They protest loudly.

Using strong ropes, Ulysses
Binds them to his ship
And orders the others to board quickly.

And to be even quicker
In moving their oars on the sea,
So as to leave behind
That accursed land,
Which makes man forget.

"Never forget those who await you.
Even if the wind blows you
To the opposite side of the world!"
Thinks Ulysses. In his mind's eye
He sees the sweet face of Penelope.

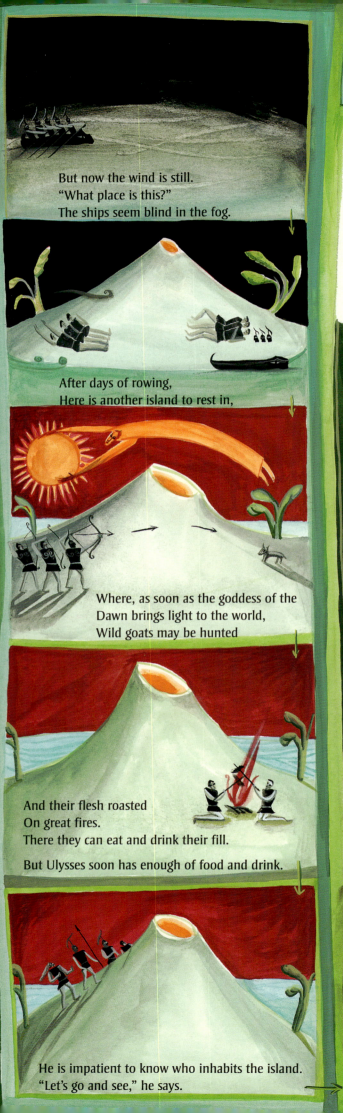

But now the wind is still.
"What place is this?"
The ships seem blind in the fog.

After days of rowing,
Here is another island to rest in,

Where, as soon as the goddess of the
Dawn brings light to the world,
Wild goats may be hunted

And their flesh roasted
On great fires.
There they can eat and drink their fill.

But Ulysses soon has enough of food and drink.

He is impatient to know who inhabits the island.
"Let's go and see," he says.

They bring with them a bag filled with wine,
The best there is, worthy of a king.
But no palaces are to be seen. Just a huge cave.
Inside, it stinks of sour milk, curdled milk. There are enormous cheeses.

WHAT ARE YOU DOING HERE?!?

"It's the home of a giant! Let's escape!"
Too late. They are caught in a trap. Polyphemus has returned
To his cave and blocked the entrance with a boulder.

We are Achaean warriors
Headed for Ithaca, having
Won the Battle of Troy.
Be hospitable with us.
Zeus will be grateful to you.

Zeus? Ha! Ha! Ha!
PUNY MAN . . . YOU DON'T KNOW
THAT I AM POLYPHEMUS.
I FEAR NO ONE.
NOT EVEN ZEUS!

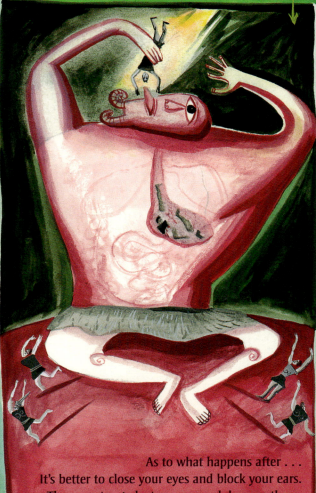

As to what happens after . . .
It's better to close your eyes and block your ears.
The monster grabs two men and devours them,
Squashing them between his teeth like a grape.

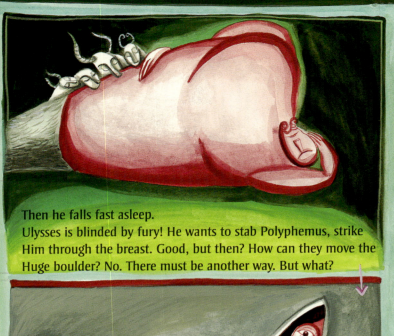

Then he falls fast asleep.
Ulysses is blinded by fury! He wants to stab Polyphemus, strike
Him through the breast. Good, but then? How can they move the
Huge boulder? No. There must be another way. But what?

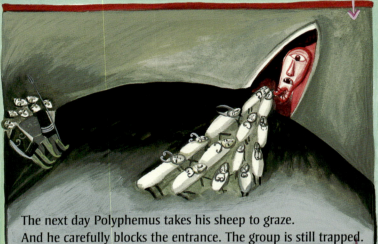

The next day Polyphemus takes his sheep to graze.
And he carefully blocks the entrance. The group is still trapped.

Ulysses notices a tree
Trunk and thinks of another trick. He orders the
Point to be sharpened, and hardened by fire.
Then he hides the weapon, now as sharp as iron.

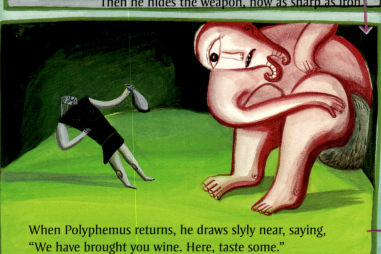

When Polyphemus returns, he draws slyly near, saying,
"We have brought you wine. Here, taste some."

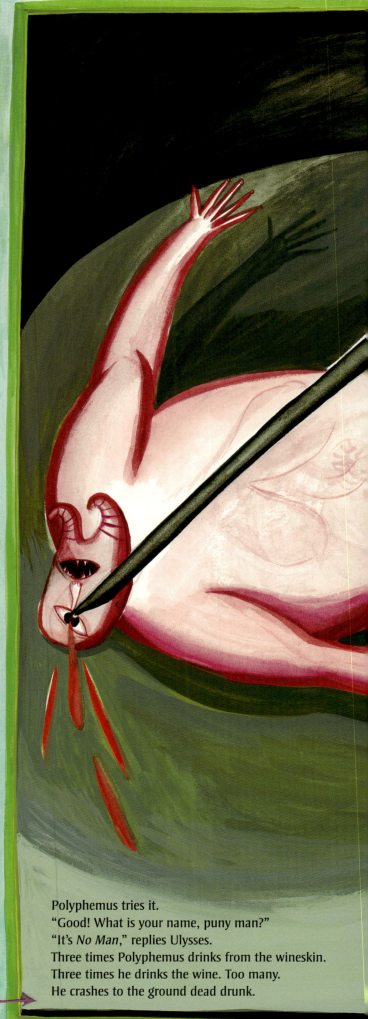

Polyphemus tries it.
"Good! What is your name, puny man?"
"It's *No Man*," replies Ulysses.
Three times Polyphemus drinks from the wineskin.
Three times he drinks the wine. Too many.
He crashes to the ground dead drunk.

The other Cyclopes run to his aid.
"Polyphemus! What's wrong? Why did you shout so?" they ask.
"*No Man* is trying to kill me!" he shouts back.
They think he is mad. Crazy. They leave.

Ulysses ties his
Men underneath
The sheep. He then
Ties himself on. The next morning Polyphemus has to
Let his sheep out. He hears them passing. He doesn't,
Of course, notice the deception.

But Ulysses makes a serious mistake.
From his ship he shouts mockingly at the Cyclops:
"Know that it was I, Ulysses, who blinded you."

From his mouth flow belches and vomit.
Dreadful to hear, dreadful to see.
But the warriors don't bother about that,
They're again busy heating the trunk on the fire.
When it is burning hot, with all their strength
They push it into the monster's sole eye.
Polyphemus utters a wild roar.
The earth shakes. The echo fills the air.

Polyphemus, furious, directs a terrible
Prayer to his father, Poseidon—he cries for revenge.
Poseidon receives his son's lament through the
Waves and vows: "I promise you I'll drive him to despair."

Yet not at once.
Much better to drive him slowly to despair,
Make him lose his way thousands of times.
Let him arrive at the Aeolean island,
At the enchanted place, the splendid palace!
And meet Aeolus too and his children as well!
There is no hurry.

The city of Aeolus, god and guardian of the winds,
At last a happy place for Ulysses and his warriors.
Lots of food and freedom of movement,
After so much weary rowing.

Aeolus wants only one thing in exchange,
Ulysses to speak and tell his story.
He asks a thousand questions a day.
"What was the Horse of Troy like?"
"And the talking horses of Achilles?"

This goes on every day for a whole month.
Until Ulysses asks leave to depart.
So Aeolus calls the storm winds,
Those that roar and blow ships off course.
He shuts them into a bag, which he ties with a silver string.

"Never open it, Ulysses! Never,
Till you've landed at Ithaca."

For nine long days Ulysses stays awake.
He checks the route.
And keeps an eye on the bag.
On the tenth day Ithaca appears on the horizon.
But Ulysses, utterly exhausted, falls asleep.

His men grab the bag.
What will be inside? Gold? Silver?
They untie the knot.
They let loose the winds.
A menacing roar, and the sky whistles
As never before.

The winds blow the ships back from
The shore. Blow them far. Very far.
The route to Ithaca is lost once more.

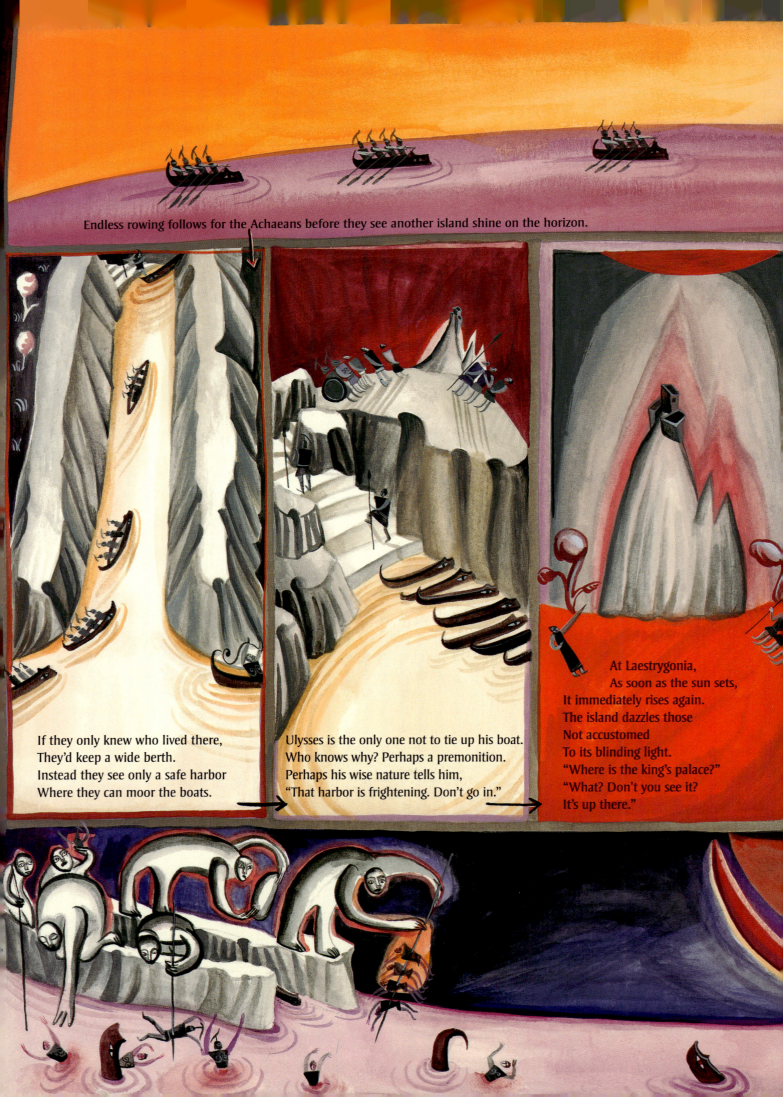

Endless rowing follows for the Achaeans before they see another island shine on the horizon.

If they only knew who lived there,
They'd keep a wide berth.
Instead they see only a safe harbor
Where they can moor the boats.

Ulysses is the only one not to tie up his boat.
Who knows why? Perhaps a premonition.
Perhaps his wise nature tells him,
"That harbor is frightening. Don't go in."

At Laestrygonia,
    As soon as the sun sets,
It immediately rises again.
The island dazzles those
Not accustomed
To its blinding light.
"Where is the king's palace?"
"What? Don't you see it?
It's up there."

The giant Antiphates is furious.
Who is frightening his wife?
Those puny men?
He grabs one and eats him.
The others run away crying,
"Ulysses! Help! Quick! Start
Moving the ships!"

Three soldiers go to see.
Inside they find a huge,
Monstrous woman.
She takes up the whole palace.
The warriors scream with horror.
The woman shouts even louder,
"Help! Antiphates!"

But Antiphates has already launched
His war cry. The other island giants are
Already at the harbor. They throw
Boulders into the sea, destroying the
Beautiful black ships. That harbor
Seemingly so safe is now a blood bath.

One ship alone is saved, the one belonging to Ulysses.
The one he had, who knows why, left outside the harbor.

"What will happen to us?" the remaining
Warriors ask. They are in despair.
Ulysses is, too. He admits as much,
"We're lost. Our only hope is to ask help from
the inhabitants of the island now before us."

But who is brave enough for that?
After what's happened . . .
Ulysses takes some sticks from his helmet.
Fate will decide.
The task falls to the group headed
By Eurylocus.

A beautiful song wafts from a palace.
The voice of a goddess.
Such a voice has never been heard.
Outside the palace strange wolves
Wag their tails.

Circe, the enchantress, appears at the entrance.
"Come in. I shall prepare you something."
A honeyed voice.
"She is too beautiful to be cruel," think the warriors.
With her immortal goddess hands
She mixes cheese and barley-meal, yellow honey and wine,
And then a powerful drug known only to her.

Eurylocus is not, however.
He hasn't trusted that goddess.
Her voice was too syrupy.
He has not entered the palace.
From outside he sees all and runs
To warn Ulysses.

Ulysses listens.
How wretched his companions are!
And poor Eurylocus who has seen
Such a terrible thing.

He grabs his sword and runs toward
Circe, the accursed one.
She must turn his men back
As they were, or he'll kill her!

The warriors are unsuspicious and drink.
"Too beautiful to be cruel."
Circe strikes them one by one with her magic wand.
Most powerful magic—they are turned into swine.

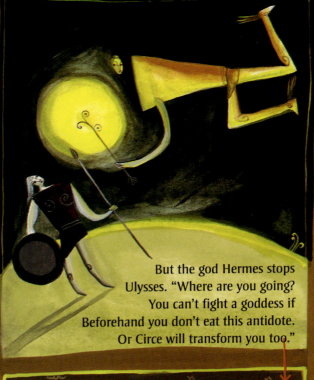

But the god Hermes stops
Ulysses. "Where are you going?
You can't fight a goddess if
Beforehand you don't eat this antidote.
Or Circe will transform you too."

The Moli plant. Black roots. White flower.
A potent drug that men
Cannot dig from the ground.
The gods can. The gods can do everything.
Ulysses thanks him.

Here now is Circe's palace.
His heart is beating like a drum.

The goddess offers him her magic potion.
But what is happening?
It doesn't work on him! He, on the contrary, tries to kill her.
How can that be? Now Circe remembers:
"An ancient prophecy told this. From the sea will come a
Strong-minded man, who will not let himself be charmed.
You must be him. You are Ulysses!"

"And you turn my men back as before," orders Ulysses.

Circe, goddess and enchantress, yields to Ulysses.
She strikes the swine lightly.
It is done, they are once more men.
And she promises to do only good magic from now on.

Circe keeps them a year by her.
She nourishes them with food and courage.
She helps them return young and strong.
Secret arts of an enchantress. They'll need them.
Circe knows that another dreadful voyage awaits them.

"Ulysses, you want to know if you will return to Ithaca.
Only Teiresias the soothsayer can tell that. But to meet
Him you must now go down to the Kingdom of the
Dead." And Circe explains how to arrive at that place,
How to cross over the thin line between life and death.

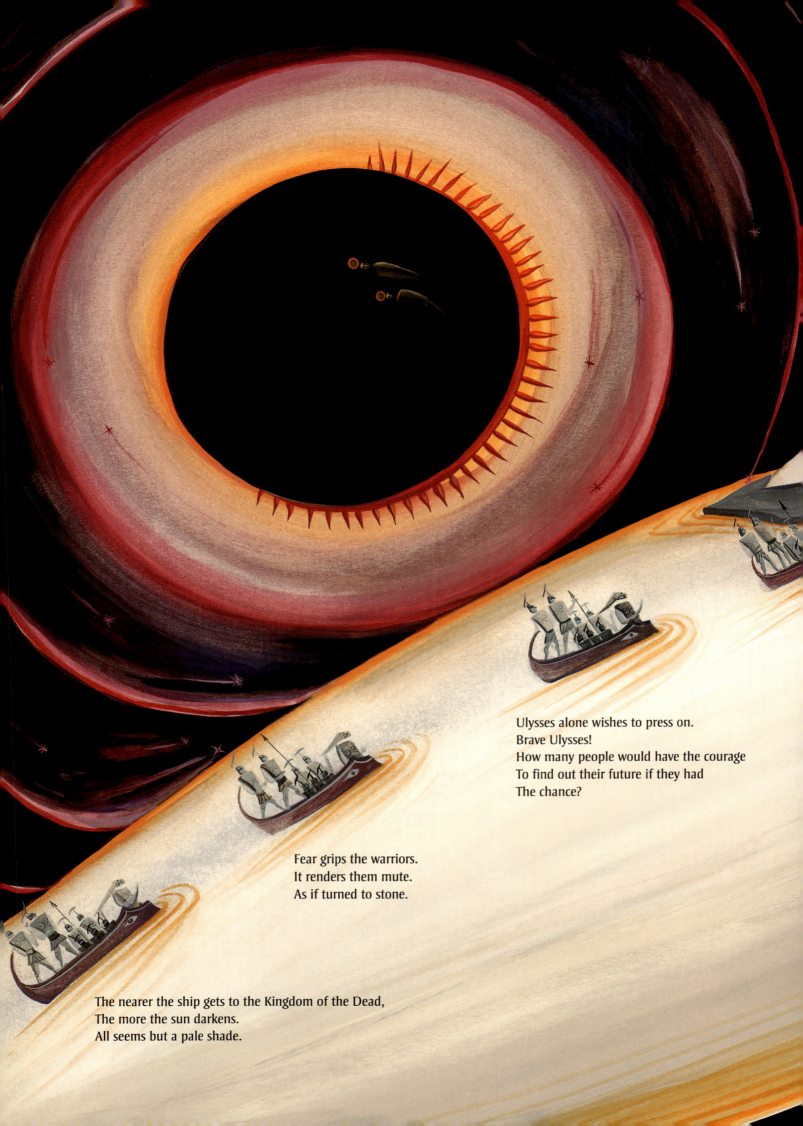

Ulysses alone wishes to press on.
Brave Ulysses!
How many people would have the courage
To find out their future if they had
The chance?

Fear grips the warriors.
It renders them mute.
As if turned to stone.

The nearer the ship gets to the Kingdom of the Dead,
The more the sun darkens.
All seems but a pale shade.

The soothsayer Teiresias awaits him already,
Where the infernal rivers meet.

Teiresias looks into his mind and prophesies,
"In your future I see two threads of fate.
If, on reaching the island of Sicily,
You kill the holy cows of the Sun god,
A terrible disaster will befall you.
If you let them live, you will return to Ithaca.
But it will not be easy. Poseidon, whose
Son Polyphemus you blinded, will do all to hinder you."

Teiresias then goes his way, leaving
Ulysses alone in the Kingdom of Death.

Brave Ulysses shivers.
Will he manage to leave this world of shades?
And will Penelope wait for him?
"Penelope is patient and faithful, and resists
Her many suitors."
It is his mother who speaks. Is she then in the
Kingdom of the Dead?
"How long have you been here, Mother?"
He wishes to embrace her, but she disappears
Like a dream.

Other women, the wives and daughters of heroes,
Appear and disappear.
The beautiful Ariadne, too.
Thanks to the thread she had given Theseus,
He, unrolling it, had entered the labyrinth.
And had escaped it, having killed the Minotaur,
The monster with a bull's head.

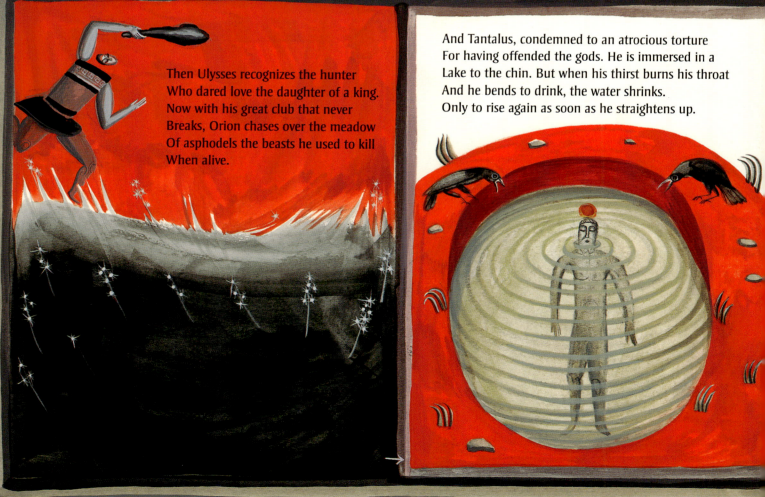

Then Ulysses recognizes the hunter
Who dared love the daughter of a king.
Now with his great club that never
Breaks, Orion chases over the meadow
Of asphodels the beasts he used to kill
When alive.

And Tantalus, condemned to an atrocious torture
For having offended the gods. He is immersed in a
Lake to the chin. But when his thirst burns his throat
And he bends to drink, the water shrinks.
Only to rise again as soon as he straightens up.

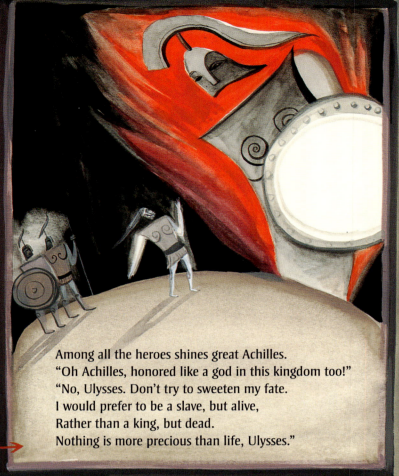

Many men now pass before Ulysses:
Commanders, warriors, all the heroes of the past.
King Agamemnon too, his friend.
"I met death not at Troy, but where I sought peace.
My treacherous wife had me killed.
Ulysses, be careful when you return to Ithaca!"

Among all the heroes shines great Achilles.
"Oh Achilles, honored like a god in this kingdom too!"
"No, Ulysses. Don't try to sweeten my fate.
I would prefer to be a slave, but alive,
Rather than a king, but dead.
Nothing is more precious than life, Ulysses."

And Sisyphus,
Condemned by the
Wrath of some god
To push a huge boulder
To the top of a mountain.
Every time he has almost got
There, a powerful force throws
It down again.

Now other souls hover around Ulysses.
They crowd about him like butterflies.
They cry shrilly like bats.
They want to speak, inquire, know.
The dead so near, so like the living.
Ulysses shivers once more.
Enough! He wants to leave.
Not stay a minute longer in this kingdom of shades!

But he knows other dangers now
Await him.
Circe has told him, before he left:
"Listen well to what you must do,
Once free of the Kingdom of the Dead.

Take some beeswax.
Spread it over the ears of your
Companions.

That will make them deaf.
So that they cannot hear.
And let the ship sail
Where fate will.

The Sirens will promise
You something impossible
For a human being:
To see at a glance everything
Happening throughout the world,
What has happened.
What will happen.

Such secrets no mortal person
Can learn without going mad."

When you coast the Island of the Sirens,
You, if you like, listen to them.
But have yourself bound to the mast.
Hands and feet.
Because the voices you will hear
Come from a superhuman world.
The Sirens, winged women-demons,
Will try to charm you.
Their song will drive you mad.
You will feel the irresistible desire
To approach them.
Do not do this, for any reason whatever.

Circe has indeed spoken true!
Ulysses, chained to the bottom of the ship,
Leaves the Island of the Sirens behind him.

Now he has another danger to face.
Circe has warned him about that, too.
Two pointed cliffs he must pass through.
One is the lair of Scylla, a sea monster
Who barks like a dog and devours sailors.

The other cliff is the home of Charybdis,
A vortex that three times a day
Vomits and swallows the green
Waters of the sea.
Woe to those who sail by
While it vomits or swallows.

"Careful, helmsman.
Don't tilt the ship!"
Ulysses warns.

But he himself makes a dreadful mistake.
He arms and awaits Scylla to strike him.
Yet Circe has told him not to provoke her.
Scylla is an immortal monster.
Stupid Ulysses! Rash man!
Scylla seizes six of his men.

Horror.
Total dismay.
Terror.
And flight.
Stupid Ulysses! Far too rash indeed!

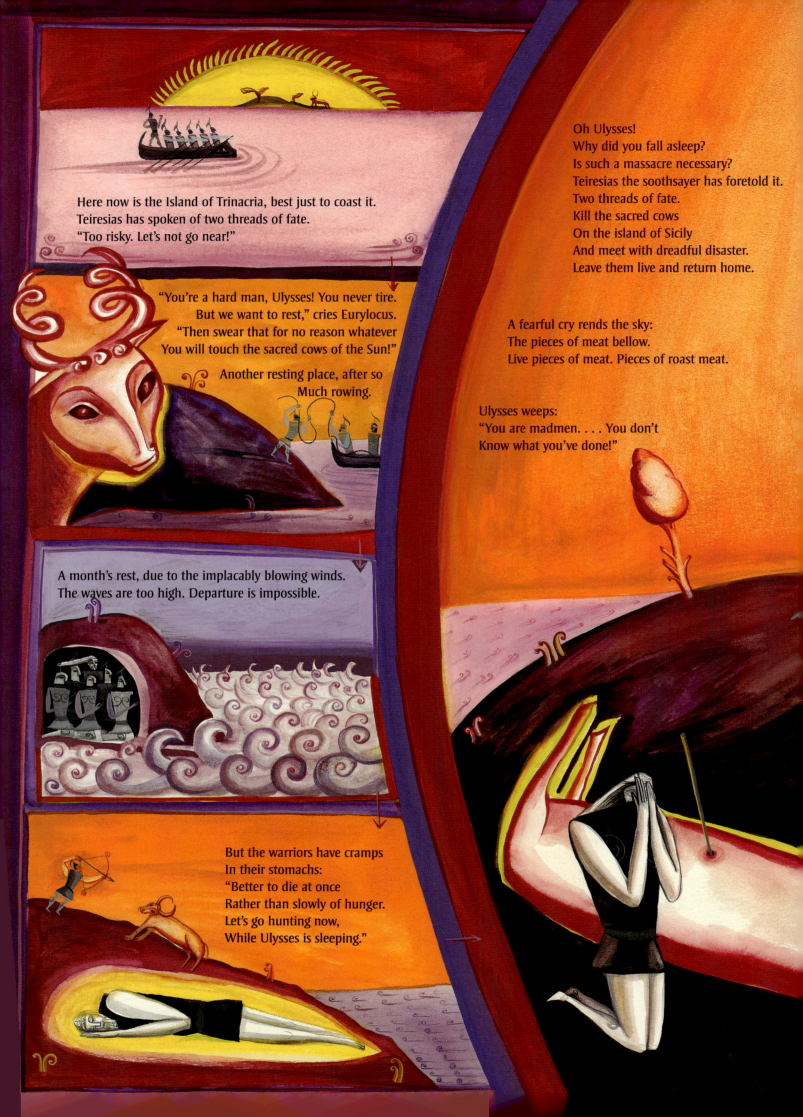

Here now is the Island of Trinacria, best just to coast it.
Teiresias has spoken of two threads of fate.
"Too risky. Let's not go near!"

"You're a hard man, Ulysses! You never tire.
But we want to rest," cries Eurylocus.
"Then swear that for no reason whatever
You will touch the sacred cows of the Sun!"

Another resting place, after so
Much rowing.

A month's rest, due to the implacably blowing winds.
The waves are too high. Departure is impossible.

But the warriors have cramps
In their stomachs:
"Better to die at once
Rather than slowly of hunger.
Let's go hunting now,
While Ulysses is sleeping."

Oh Ulysses!
Why did you fall asleep?
Is such a massacre necessary?
Teiresias the soothsayer has foretold it.
Two threads of fate.
Kill the sacred cows
On the island of Sicily
And meet with dreadful disaster.
Leave them live and return home.

A fearful cry rends the sky:
The pieces of meat bellow.
Live pieces of meat. Pieces of roast meat.

Ulysses weeps:
"You are madmen. . . . You don't
Know what you've done!"

The ear of the Sun god hears all from on high.
His eye sees all.
His adored cows! Slaughtered . . .

"Punish them, Zeus! Don't let them depart! I want revenge!
If not I'll stop giving mortals light."
"I'll wreck the ships of Ulysses with a bolt of lightning," promises Zeus.

And that is what he does.

Hanging on to the ship's mast, Ulysses tries to save his life.
Only he is left.
His remaining companions have plunged to the depths of the sea.

Nine days long he rows with tired arms.
Till he reaches the island of Calypso,
Goddess and beautiful nymph.

She takes care of him like a son.
She loves him as a husband.
This continues for seven years.

She doesn't want him to leave:
"Stay with me, Ulysses. I will make you immortal.
Penelope will soon be old
And you, at her side, just a weak man."

Immortality. To live forever.
Life is dear to man because death exists.
No.
Ulysses wants to return to Ithaca.

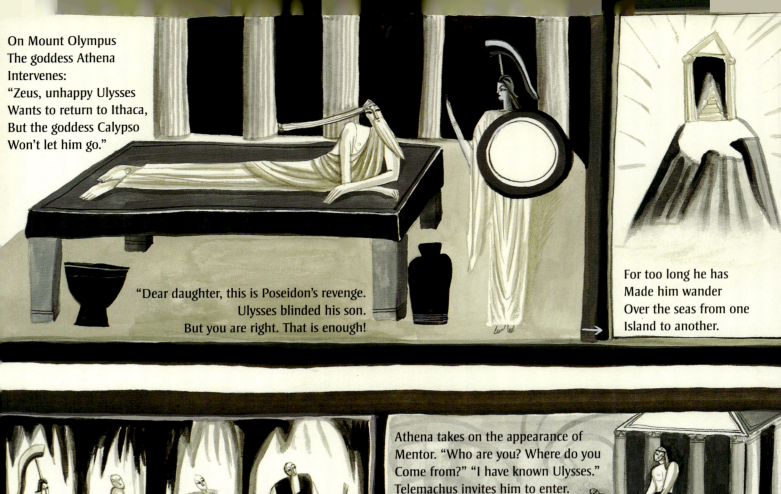

On Mount Olympus
The goddess Athena
Intervenes:
"Zeus, unhappy Ulysses
Wants to return to Ithaca,
But the goddess Calypso
Won't let him go."

"Dear daughter, this is Poseidon's revenge.
Ulysses blinded his son.
But you are right. That is enough!

For too long he has
Made him wander
Over the seas from one
Island to another.

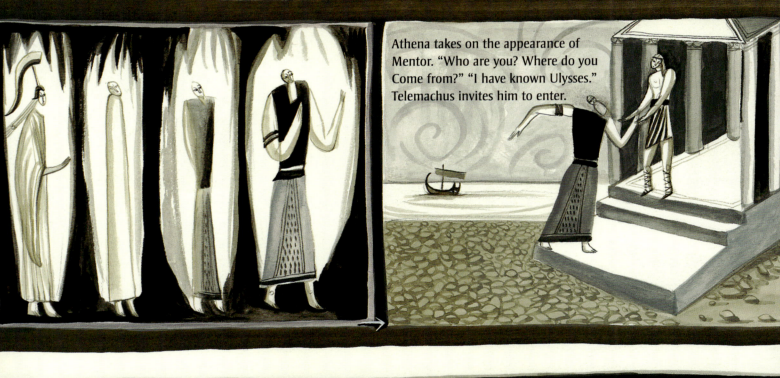

Athena takes on the appearance of
Mentor. "Who are you? Where do you
Come from?" "I have known Ulysses."
Telemachus invites him to enter.

What do you mean?! It is Penelope who's the clever culprit.
Your mother tricks us. She has promised to marry one of us
As soon as she has finished weaving a great cloth.
And she does weave by day.
But at night she secretly undoes it.

Yes, Penelope is playing for time.
She always hopes that Ulysses will return.

"Thank you, Father.
I shall make straight
For Ithaca."

I wish first of all
To speak to his son,
Telemachus.

He is young, he
Needs courage!"

Poseidon must
Still his wrath.
Such is my will.
And you Athena, go,
Help Ulysses!"

What troubles you, young Telemachus?
Your eyes are so sad.

They are the cause! The suitors! Proud and arrogant.
They come into my house. Eat and drink their fill.
Court my mother. Lay traps for her.
Oh, if only Ulysses were here!

Telemachus, go and seek word of your father.
If he is reported dead, you will tell your
Mother to marry again.

Then Mentor disappears,
Transformed into a swift bird.
Telemachus understands:

"It was a god!"
Now, in his heart, is the
Courage instilled by Athena.

So Telemachus, who has never seen anywhere except Ithaca,
Is now ready to set sail.
Who knows what news he will hear from his father's old friends.

Here is Pylos, the kingdom of Nestor.
He has fought at Troy with Ulysses.
If he knows anything, he will tell it.

He comes to King Menelaus
Full of hope.

Menelaus receives him with joy.
"I am happy to embrace you, son of Ulysses.
Among all the friends I lost at Troy, your father
Is the one I miss most, the man who, through
His cleverness, overcame the enemy.

"Go, Hermes! Fly to the goddess Calypso!
Tell her to dissolve her ties with Ulysses.
Tell her this is an order from Zeus."

"I'm sorry. I have no news.
Once the war was over, everyone set off in their own ships.
I soon returned home. I don't know anything about Ulysses.

Go to Menelaus. He too was with us at Troy.
Perhaps he has heard something."
Telemachus sets off for Sparta.

But he is not dead. I know this for certain.
The goddess Calypso holds him prisoner.
I was told this by Proteus, a god of the sea.
Ulysses weeps and despairs. With all his heart
He wishes to return to Ithaca."

On Mount Olympus the gods also speak about Ulysses.
They want to settle his case, once and for all.
Calypso is to let him leave.
He is to return home at last.

Hermes whispers
The divine command
To Calypso.

The goddess is sad,
But must obey.
"You are free, Ulysses.
I'll give you tools
To build a raft."

Ulysses works
Day and night,

Till the raft is ready.
At last he can depart.

For seventeen days the raft rides like a
Cork on the sea. Ulysses is alone. He has
Nothing left. He is no longer anything,
Neither hero, nor husband, and not even
Father. He is only a tiny man on the infinite
Sea. Never in his life has he felt so lost.

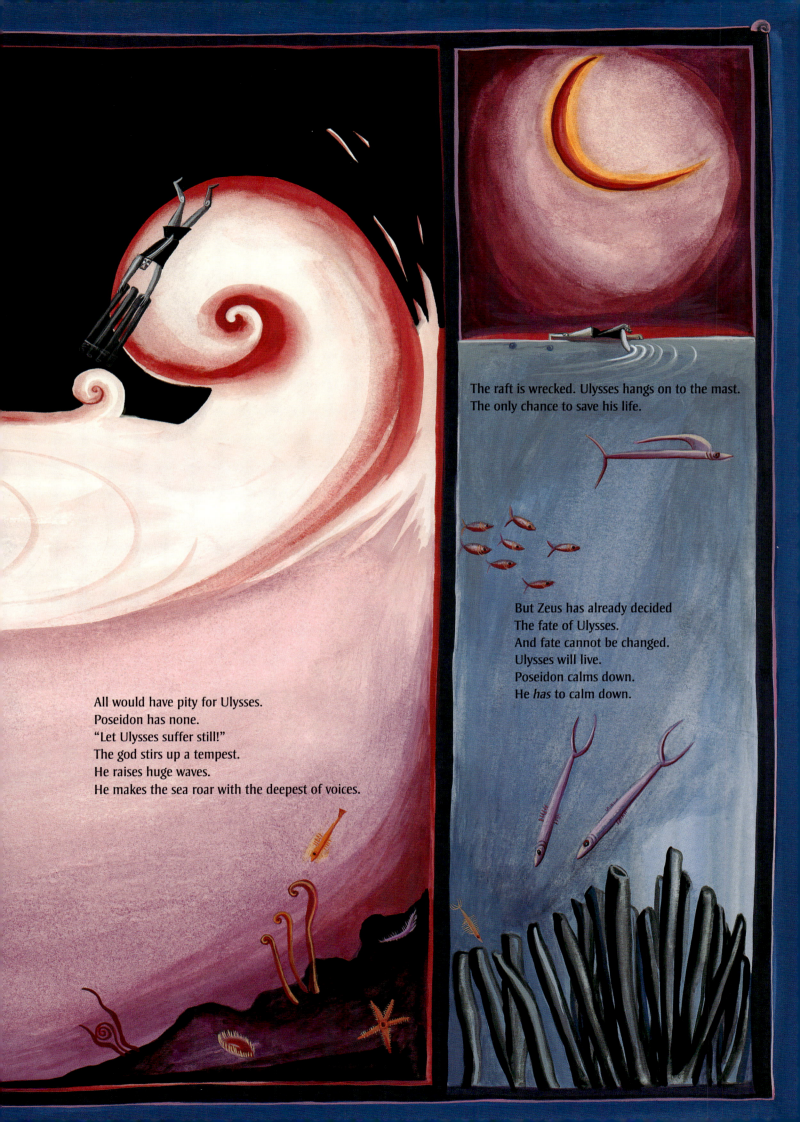

All would have pity for Ulysses.
Poseidon has none.
"Let Ulysses suffer still!"
The god stirs up a tempest.
He raises huge waves.
He makes the sea roar with the deepest of voices.

The raft is wrecked. Ulysses hangs on to the mast.
The only chance to save his life.

But Zeus has already decided
The fate of Ulysses.
And fate cannot be changed.
Ulysses will live.
Poseidon calms down.
He *has* to calm down.

Ulysses approaches the land of the Phaeacians.
So Zeus has decreed.
For that is the island of peace,
Where he can recover his forces.

A tumbling river enters the sea.
"Have pity on me. Calm your current
And let me land," supplicates Ulysses.

The river god calms the current,
Allows Ulysses to enter the land
Of the generous Phaeacians, then lays him,
Exhausted, on the shore.

Never has a man been so tired.
Ulysses falls dead asleep
On a bed of leaves.

In the meantime Athena goes to Nausicaa, the daughter of the king of
The Phaeacians, and speaks to her in a dream:

"Nausicaa, wash and prepare your wedding garments.
The day of your marriage is at hand."

On waking, Nausicaa is astonished at the dream.
So clear and present to her.
"Yet it cannot be only the fruit of my imagination."

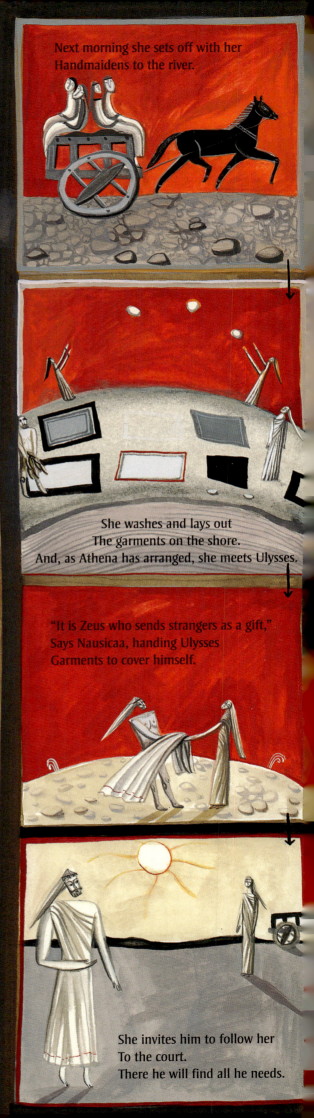

Next morning she sets off with her
Handmaidens to the river.

She washes and lays out
The garments on the shore.
And, as Athena has arranged, she meets Ulysses.

"It is Zeus who sends strangers as a gift,"
Says Nausicaa, handing Ulysses
Garments to cover himself.

She invites him to follow her
To the court.
There he will find all he needs.

Ulysses follows Nausicaa's cart.
Something within him says:
"Trust her."

Here is the palace,
With golden doors, silver doorposts,
Turquoise enamel, bronze walls.
A wonder to see.

Ulysses tells his story to the king,
That he has been a hero, a husband, and father.
He tells of the War of Troy,
Of his many misadventures
While trying to return
Home.

The Phaeacians possess magic boats
That read in the mind exactly where to go.
So they cannot mistake the route.
Indestructible.
Therefore no storm can wreck them.
Ulysses, this time, is sure of returning home.
He stretches down on a soft carpet
And abandons himself to a sweet, deep sleep.

Ulysses is still sleeping when the
Phaeacians lay him on the beach
Of Ithaca.

Home at last!

But he cannot run at once to Penelope.
At the court the suitors would kill him in an instant.

And Athena knows this:
"To regain what
Is yours, Ulysses,
Do not use force.
Sharpen the weapon
Of your intelligence.
Only thus will you
Be the master when
Facing the enemy.
You have this weapon,
And I shall help you.

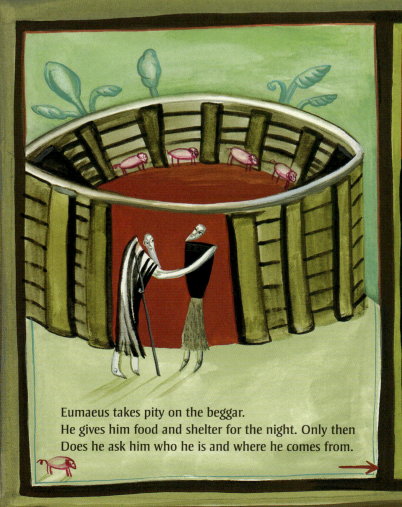

Eumaeus takes pity on the beggar.
He gives him food and shelter for the night. Only then
Does he ask him who he is and where he comes from.

Ulysses recounts, but not his true story.
It is too soon to reveal his identity!

You, Ulysses,
Great king of Ithaca, will enter
Your home as a stranger,
In the guise of a beggar.

Unrecognized, you can observe everyone,
Discover who is on your side, and secretly
Prepare your plot. Go to the swineherd
Eumaeus, who has always been faithful to you.
I, in the meantime, will go to Sparta, to fetch
Your son Telemachus."

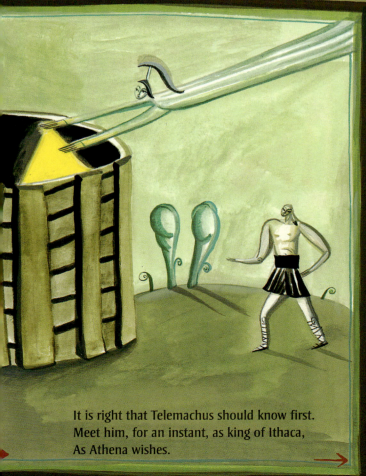

It is right that Telemachus should know first.
Meet him, for an instant, as king of Ithaca,
As Athena wishes.

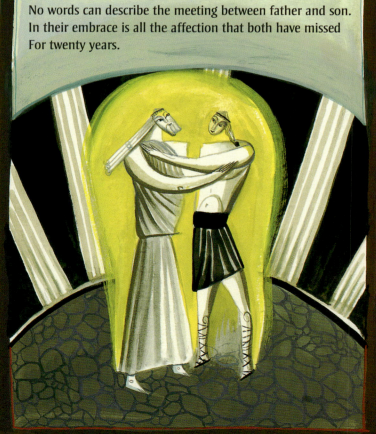

No words can describe the meeting between father and son.
In their embrace is all the affection that both have missed
For twenty years.

After the embrace begin the father's questions
To the son, the son's to the father.
Ulysses, do you want to know about Penelope,
About the situation at court?
How many suitors are there?
How many weapons have they?
How many lances?
How many swords?
Then he tells him of his plan.

Telemachus learns the arts of Ulysses.
Patience. Calmness.
The mind cold and lucid.
Perfect reasoning and calculation.
Only afterward they move into action.

For now the secret must be kept.
Return to court as if nothing has happened.
Don't tell anyone that Ulysses has returned.

Not even Penelope.
Not yet.
She has been awaiting him twenty years, it is true,
Weaving and undoing the cloth,
But it is better that Ulysses defeat the suitors first.
And anyway, who knows if she would recognize him?

Only his old dog Argo knows him.
His beggar's garb does not deceive Argo.
He sits down at his feet immediately.

At court everything happens
As Ulysses has thought.
The suitors are arrogant,
Treacherous, violent.
They insult him.

"Shame!" says Penelope indignantly.
The suitors stop,
Remain silent.
Not because of her anger,
But because her beauty leaves them breathless.

The power of Athena is the cause.
With a divine unguent she has made
Penelope's skin fairer than ivory.

Athena wants the suitors to court her,
To bring her wedding gifts.
All this is part of her plan:
That they should give back what for years
They have been stealing at court!

Jewels as bright as yellow suns,
A golden necklace with amber beads,
Two earrings,
And a peplum embroidered in gold.

But these gifts do not brighten her gaze.
Penelope, sad, withdraws to her rooms.

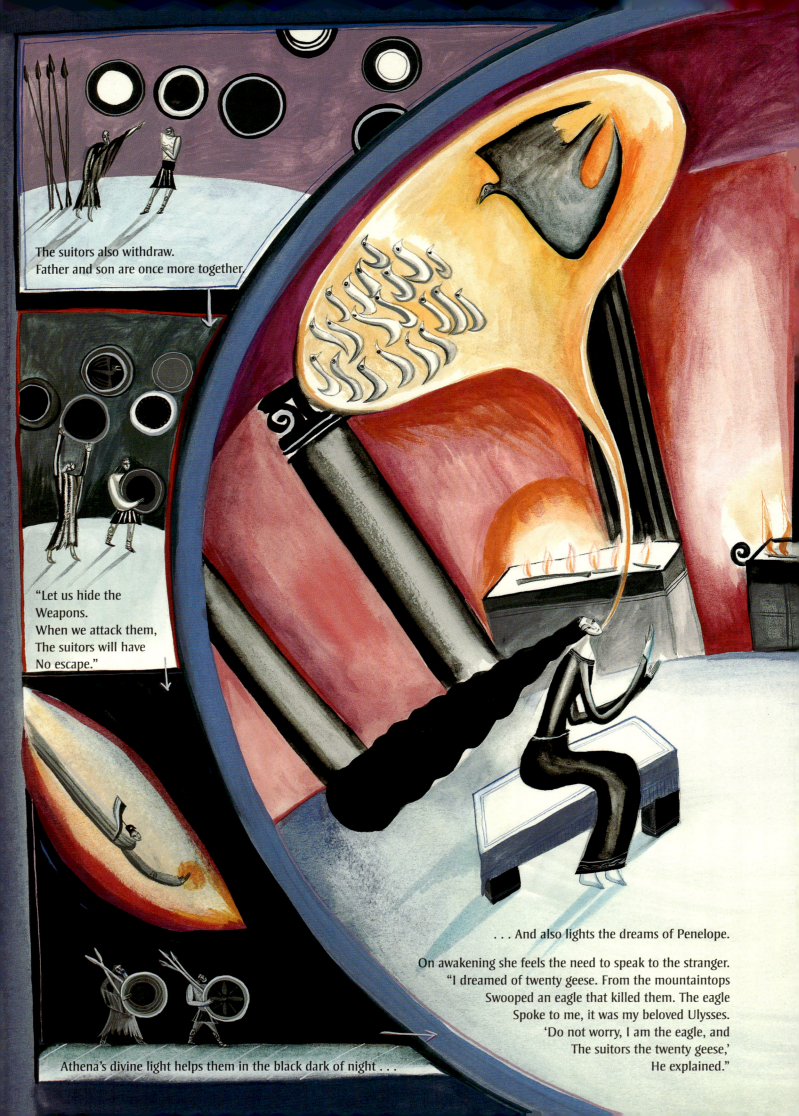

The suitors also withdraw.
Father and son are once more together.

"Let us hide the
Weapons.
When we attack them,
The suitors will have
No escape."

Athena's divine light helps them in the black dark of night . . .

. . . And also lights the dreams of Penelope.

On awakening she feels the need to speak to the stranger.
"I dreamed of twenty geese. From the mountaintops
Swooped an eagle that killed them. The eagle
Spoke to me, it was my beloved Ulysses.
'Do not worry, I am the eagle, and
The suitors the twenty geese,'
He explained."

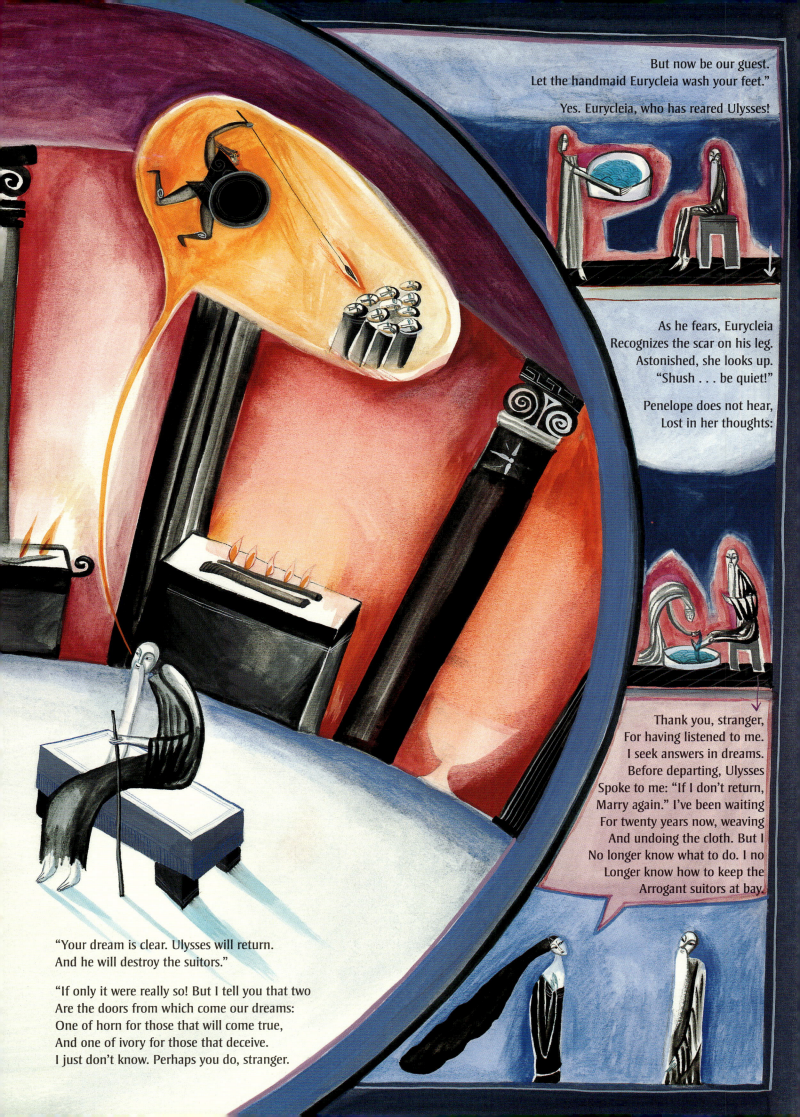

But now be our guest.
Let the handmaid Eurycleia wash your feet."

Yes. Eurycleia, who has reared Ulysses!

As he fears, Eurycleia
Recognizes the scar on his leg.
Astonished, she looks up.
"Shush . . . be quiet!"

Penelope does not hear,
Lost in her thoughts:

Thank you, stranger,
For having listened to me.
I seek answers in dreams.
Before departing, Ulysses
Spoke to me: "If I don't return,
Marry again." I've been waiting
For twenty years now, weaving
And undoing the cloth. But I
No longer know what to do. I no
Longer know how to keep the
Arrogant suitors at bay.

"Your dream is clear. Ulysses will return.
And he will destroy the suitors."

"If only it were really so! But I tell you that two
Are the doors from which come our dreams:
One of horn for those that will come true,
And one of ivory for those that deceive.
I just don't know. Perhaps you do, stranger.

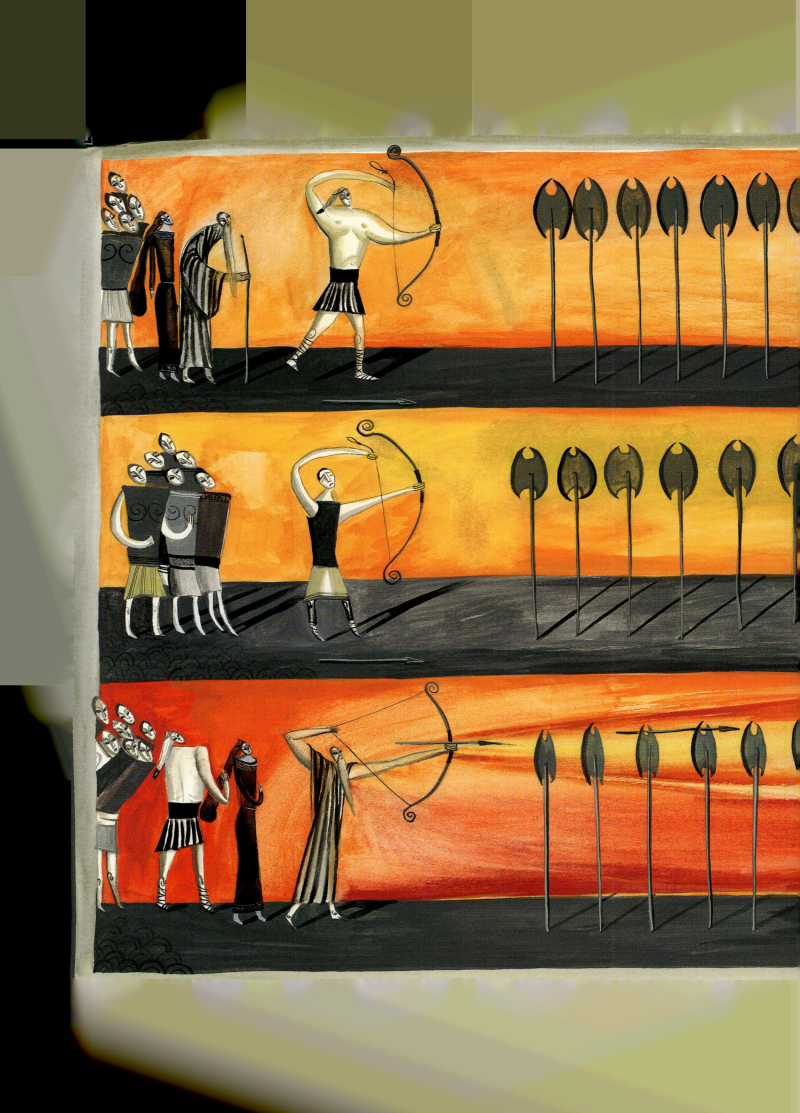

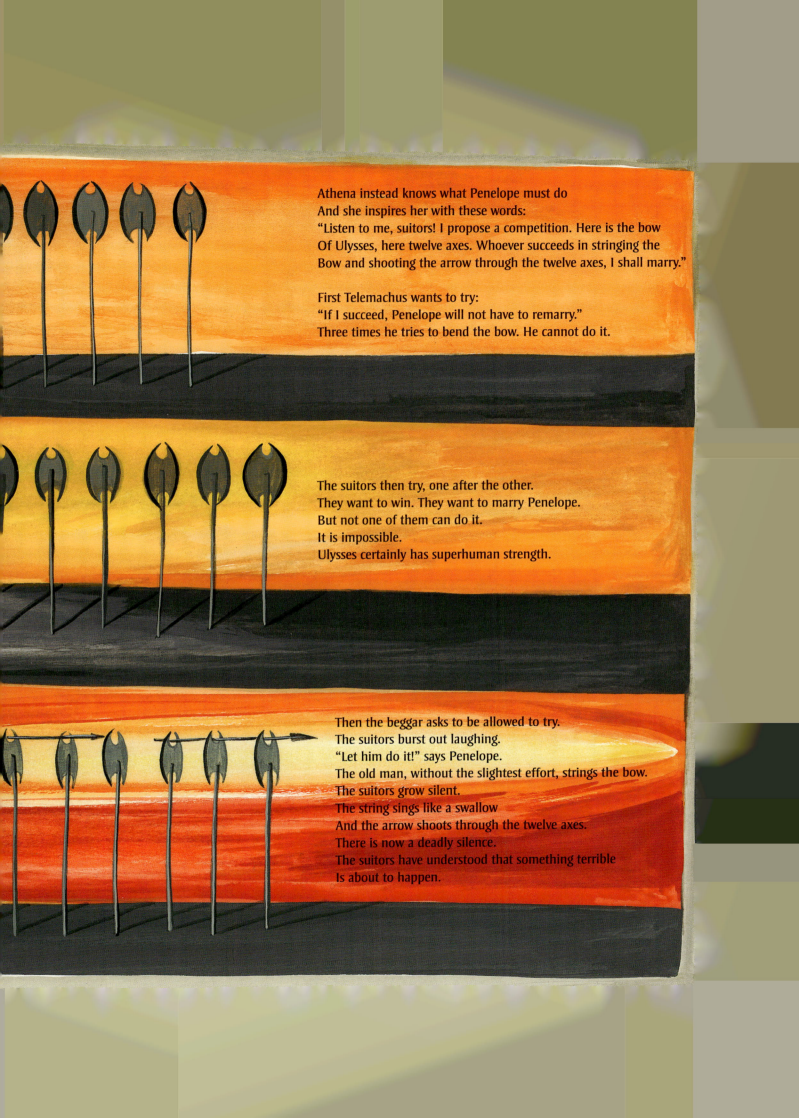

Athena instead knows what Penelope must do
And she inspires her with these words:
"Listen to me, suitors! I propose a competition. Here is the bow
Of Ulysses, here twelve axes. Whoever succeeds in stringing the
Bow and shooting the arrow through the twelve axes, I shall marry."

First Telemachus wants to try:
"If I succeed, Penelope will not have to remarry."
Three times he tries to bend the bow. He cannot do it.

The suitors then try, one after the other.
They want to win. They want to marry Penelope.
But not one of them can do it.
It is impossible.
Ulysses certainly has superhuman strength.

Then the beggar asks to be allowed to try.
The suitors burst out laughing.
"Let him do it!" says Penelope.
The old man, without the slightest effort, strings the bow.
The suitors grow silent.
The string sings like a swallow
And the arrow shoots through the twelve axes.
There is now a deadly silence.
The suitors have understood that something terrible
Is about to happen.

But they have no weapons to defend themselves.
And Eumaeus has closed all the exits.
There is no escape for the suitors.

When all is over, the old beggar
Can return to being Ulysses, king of Ithaca . . .

. . . And the husband of Penelope,
So long awaited. In their embrace is
All the love both have missed
For twenty years.

But already the relatives of the dead suitors
Swarm in front of the court.
"Revenge!" is their sole cry.

Athena, quick-witted, flies to Zeus:
"Father! It will be another slaughter!
What do we want for mankind?
Always war, or peace at last?"

My dear daughter, you are right.
It is time for mankind to live in peace,
And that we gods let Ulysses reign.
I shall give forgetfulness to all
So that they will forget
Their dead fathers, sons, and brothers.

Athena flies swiftly down from the heavens:
"Stop! There has been enough bloodshed!"
The goddess's voice is very powerful.
All the weapons fall to the ground.

"You too, Ulysses, must stop if you do not want Zeus to be angry!"

Ulysses obeys.
He is happy to do so.
All is well.
Peace.

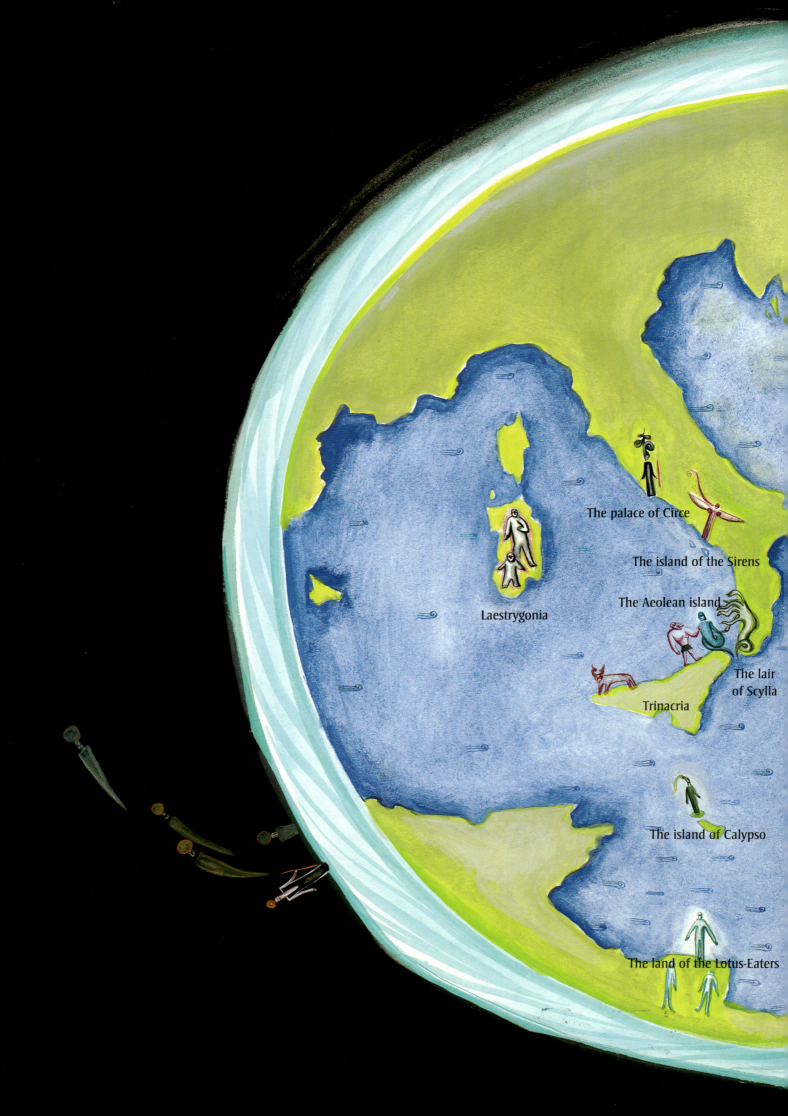

The palace of Circe

The island of the Sirens

The Aeolean island

Laestrygonia

The lair
of Scylla

Trinacria

The island of Calypso

The land of the Lotus-Eaters